Fairy Bears
Blossom

"I promise to do my best. I promise to work hard to care for the world and all its plants, animals and children. This is the Fairy Bear Promise."

Look out for more friendly Fairy Bears!

Dizzy

Sunny

Blossom

Sparkle

Primrose

Misty

Lulu

Poppy

Visit the secret world of the Fairy Bears and
explore the magical Crystal Caves . . .

www.fairybearsworld.com

Fairy Bears

Blossom

Julie Sykes

Illustrated by Samantha Chaffey

MACMILLAN CHILDREN'S BOOKS

First published 2010 by Macmillan Children's Books
a division of Macmillan Publishers Limited
20 New Wharf Road, London N1 9RR
Basingstoke and Oxford
Associated companies throughout the world
www.panmacmillan.com

ISBN 978-0-330-51203-9

Text copyright © Julie Sykes 2010
Illustrations copyright © Samantha Chaffey 2010

The right of Julie Sykes and Samantha Chaffey to be identified as the
author and illustrator of this work has been asserted by them in
accordance with the Copyright, Designs and Patents Act 1988.

All rights reserved. No part of this publication may be
reproduced, stored in or introduced into a retrieval system, or
transmitted, in any form or by any means (electronic, mechanical,
photocopying, recording or otherwise), without the prior written
permission of the publisher. Any person who does any unauthorized
act in relation to this publication may be liable to criminal
prosecution and civil claims for damages.

1 3 5 7 9 8 6 4 2

A CIP catalogue record for this book is available from
the British Library.

Printed and bound in the UK by CPI Mackays, Chatham ME5 8TD

This book is sold subject to the condition that it shall not,
by way of trade or otherwise, be lent, resold, hired out,
or otherwise circulated without the publisher's prior consent
in any form of binding or cover other than that in which
it is published and without a similar condition including this
condition being imposed on the subsequent purchaser.

For Alistair

Firefly Meadow
Sycamore
GRAND DOOR
Caves for Fairy Bears who work for King & Queen
Turquoise Chamber
Diamond Arch
To The Royal Caves
ROYAL TUNNEL
MAIN TUNNEL
Whispering Pool
Rocky Island
Rowing Lake
Honey Bridge

Tree
Firefly Meadow
Nectar Cave
Diamond Dell
Starlight Cave
Crystal Maze
Hospital Cave
Ruby Grotto
School Caves
Air Ball Stadium
To The Home Caves
Play park
Underground Stream
To Royal Theatre

Prologue

At the bottom of Firefly Meadow, not far from the stream, stands a tall sycamore tree. The tree is old with a thick grey trunk and spreading branches. Hidden amongst the branches is a forgotten squirrel hole. If you could fly through the squirrel hole and down the inside of the tree's hollow trunk, you would find a secret door that leads to a special place. Open the door and step inside the magical Crystal Caves, home of the Fairy Bears.

The Fairy Bears are always busy. They work hard caring for nature and children everywhere. You'll have to be quick to see them, and you'll have to believe in magic.

Fairy Bears

Do you believe in Fairy Bear magic?
Can you keep a secret? Then come on in –
the Fairy Bears would love to meet you.

Chapter One

The noise coming from the class cave was deafening as timid Blossom went inside and looked around anxiously for someone she knew. Her friend Sparkle hadn't arrived yet and Dizzy and Sunny were chattering with a large group of Fairy Bears. Blossom hesitated, feeling too shy to join the group. Across the cave the magic mirror seemed to wink at her. Blossom stared at it and the mirror winked again. Was it calling her over? Shyly, Blossom went and looked into the rectangular glass surrounded by tiny

crystals, and blushed as
her own face stared
back at her. She
was a small
Fairy Bear
with pretty
pale-gold fur,
pink wings,
big brown eyes
and a button black nose.
Her reflection blushed too, then quickly
faded to be replaced by a slim girl with
curly brown hair pulled into an untidy
ponytail. The girl was acting on a stage but
she didn't seem to be enjoying herself. Her
face was tense and she held her body stiffly.

"Poor thing," whispered Blossom, feeling
her own stomach flutter nervously in
sympathy.

The picture faded in a swirl of pink mist

and was replaced with an image of Coral.
Blossom spun round, wondering if Coral
had seen the nervous-looking girl too, but
to her surprise she was alone. Coral was on
the other side of the class combing her pure-
white fur with a bored expression on her face.

Miss Alaska came into the room and
the Fairy Bears scurried to their seats.
Sparkle had arrived and Blossom sat down
gratefully next to her friend.

"Good morning, class," said Miss Alaska,
smiling. "Today I have chosen another
Fairy Bear to go out on a task."

The Fairy Bears rustled their wings in
excitement. The tasks were very important.
You had to pass them all to be allowed to
move up to the senior class. Miss Alaska
was working her way through the junior
class, choosing one Fairy Bear at a time to
perform their first task.

It's going to be Coral, thought Blossom, remembering the pictures in the magic mirror. Coral loved acting so she would probably be asked to help the girl with the curly hair.

"Before I tell you who I've picked, let's say the Fairy Bear Promise. Blossom, are you with us or are you enjoying a lovely daydream?"

The class laughed and Blossom blushed, her pale-gold cheeks suddenly matching the pink of her wings. She laid her wand on her stone desk and, folding her wings behind her, held Sparkle and Sunny's paws. With tightly closed eyes Blossom began to chant.

"I promise to do my best. I promise to work hard to care for the world and all its plants, animals and children. This is the Fairy Bear Promise."

When she opened her eyes Miss Alaska
was holding up a sycamore leaf. The class
cave was so silent Blossom
could hear the moon clock
whirring softly on the
cave wall.

"Congratulations,
Blossom! Today you

are going out on your first task!" said Miss
Alaska dramatically.

"Hooray!" cheered Sparkle and Sunny
loudly.

"*Me?*" squeaked Blossom in alarm.

"Yes, you," replied Miss Alaska kindly.
She handed Blossom the sycamore leaf.
"Your task is written here."

Blossom quickly read the task and then
reread it to check she'd got the details right.

"It's a good-luck task," she shyly
announced. "I must sprinkle a girl called
Chloe with good-luck stars. She's acting
the part of Alice in a play called *Alice
in Wonderland*. It's the lead role. Chloe
wasn't meant to be the star. She was the
understudy, but the girl who was playing
Alice broke her ankle in a roller-skating
accident."

"Why did Blossom get that task?" called

out Coral. "She doesn't know anything about acting. I'm the best actress in the school."

Blossom's wings quivered. Perhaps there had been a mistake? But Miss Alaska didn't think so.

"This task is for Blossom," she said firmly. "Don't forget to test your wand before you start. Good luck, Blossom."

Hesitantly Blossom picked up her wand. It was silver with a pink diamond set in the star at the wand's tip. The wand was new, a present from her mum and dad for her birthday last month, and Blossom was still getting used to it.

"Go on," said Sparkle encouragingly.

Tightly gripping the wand, Blossom waved it in the air. There was a loud squeak and then a stream of pink stars floated out from the tip. The stars seemed to dance in the air as they formed a picture.

"A mouse!" exclaimed Blossom.

The pink star mouse flicked its tail and then evaporated. The class roared with laughter and clapped. Blossom blushed with pleasure as she walked to the cave door.

"Squeak, squeak!" said Coral spitefully as Blossom passed her. "Blossom the timid mouse. You won't pass this task. Even your wand knows you're not brave enough to complete it."

"Yes I am," protested Blossom. But Blossom's insides were trembling like butterfly wings in a storm. Did she really have the courage to solve her first task?

Chapter Two

Clutching her wand in one paw and the sycamore leaf in the other, Blossom flew out of the school caves towards the Main Tunnel. It was busy with grown-up Fairy Bears going out for the day and Blossom hovered for ages in the side tunnel waiting for a gap big enough for her to fly out and join them, too shy to push in. Her journey ended at the foot of the gnarled root staircase that led to the Grand Door, the main way in and out of the sycamore tree that hid the Crystal Caves. Blossom waited patiently at the back of the queue for her turn to climb the staircase, but each time she got closer to the stairs she was squeezed back again by the jostling crowd. At last she gave up, deciding to wait for the crowd to disappear.

"Hello, are you all right?"

At first Blossom didn't realize the friendly-looking Fairy Bear with chocolate-coloured fur and green wings was talking to her.

"I'm Racer," he said. "You're in Miss Alaska's class, aren't you? Are you going out on your first task?"

Blossom nodded. She'd seen Racer around the school. He was a popular Fairy Bear in the seniors and often went out on tasks. Managing to find her voice she said quietly, "I'm Blossom."

"You'll never get your turn hanging back

like that," said Racer. "You have to be
more confident. Stick with me and I'll show
you what to do."

Blossom joined Racer at the back of the

queue. Each time someone knocked into
him he didn't wobble or step back. Blossom
copied him, keeping close to his side, and
soon it was their turn to climb the staircase.
Racer bounced up the stairs two at a time
and vanished through the enormous Grand
Door. Blossom followed, but then stopped
inside the tree trunk, blinking rapidly as her
eyes adjusted to the dark.

"Boo!" said Racer, chuckling as Blossom
jumped. "I thought I'd wait for you, seeing
as it's your first time. You look nervous."

"I am," Blossom admitted.

"Well, don't be," said Racer,
encouragingly. "Once you get started,
you'll be fine. The tasks are great fun."

"Thanks!" Blossom felt more confident
as she flew up the inside of the tree with
Racer. There were Fairy Bears all around
her, their wings humming musically as they

15

flew towards the pale circle of light shining through the squirrel hole near the top of the tree.

It was a beautiful day outside. The stream sparkled in the sunlight and Firefly Meadow was bursting with colourful flowers. Racer somersaulted in delight.

"Good luck, Blossom! You can't fail on a day like this."

Dipping his green wings in a goodbye salute, he sped off across the meadow. Watching him go, Blossom suddenly felt less confident. Why had Miss Alaska picked her for this task? Blossom was hopeless at acting. And she didn't feel ready to go out on her own. Should she turn back and ask Miss Alaska to give the task to someone else?

"I can't do that!" said Blossom suddenly. Giving up before she'd even tried would mean failing her first task and staying in Miss Alaska's class for another year. It would also mean failing Chloe. Remembering Chloe's worried face gave Blossom courage.

Blossom hovered in the air while she studied the map on the sycamore leaf. She carefully remembered the directions before wrapping the leaf tightly round her wand. Chloe was acting in a small theatre on the edge of a town. It was a long way from the Crystal Caves.

"Chloe, here I come," said Blossom, flying across the stream at the bottom of the meadow.

Blossom usually loved flying, but today she was too nervous to enjoy it. The closer she came to the theatre, the more uncomfortable she felt. Her tummy was fizzing like a fireworks display and her wings tingled. It was exhausting! Flying over a park, a few streets away from the theatre, Blossom was tempted to soar down for a rest. The park was green and inviting, with lots of bushes and trees. Blossom hesitated but then continued on her way, scared that if she stopped she might not have the courage to go on with her journey.

Minutes later she arrived. The theatre's huge glass windows and doors were all tightly shut. Blossom hovered outside, wondering how to get in. Opening doors by magic took a lot of energy, and Blossom wasn't strong enough to do it yet. Maybe there was a back entrance? Blossom flew over the building to the car park behind. A man was vigorously sweeping the pavement. Behind him, the theatre's back door was propped open with a chair. Unseen, Blossom dived through the door and into a long corridor that had more doors on either side.

"Dressing rooms," said Blossom.

Miss Alaska had taken them on a tour of the Royal Theatre in the Crystal Caves and they'd seen dressing rooms there. Some of the doors were open and Blossom flew in and out of the rooms until she reached the last door. It was ajar and Blossom could hear a girl talking inside. Was it Chloe? Quietly she flew into the room, keeping close to the ceiling so she wouldn't be noticed. Blossom recognized Chloe immediately from her picture in the magic mirror. She was standing in the middle of the room, wearing a blue dress with a sparkling white apron, rehearsing her lines.

"Curiouser and curiouser," said Chloe, holding out her arms. "I seem to be stretching. Goodbye feet . . ."

Chloe acted out her body growing taller, cricking her neck sidewise as her head hit an imaginary ceiling. Blossom was transfixed. Not wanting to miss a second of Chloe's amazing acting, she fluttered closer and landed on the dressing-table mirror.

"What's that?" said Chloe, stepping forward. "Oh!" she gasped, covering her mouth with her hands in surprise.

Suddenly Blossom realized that Chloe had stopped acting and was looking straight at her.

"Am I dreaming?" Chloe asked hesitantly. "What are you?"

Blossom's wings went ice cold as Chloe's

face came nearer. If Blossom was braver, she could have reached out and touched Chloe on the nose with her wand.

"I thought you were a bee but you're not, are you? You look like . . ." Chloe hesitated. "You look like a little bear with wings."

"Hello," squeaked Blossom, struggling to find her voice. "I'm a Fairy Bear. My name's Blossom."

Chapter Three

Blossom explained about Fairy Bears as Chloe listened, enthralled.

"And we help animals, plants and children who need us," she finished up, twirling her wand.

Chloe looked like she might burst with excitement. "Why are you here? Are you going to help someone?"

Blossom was about to answer her when she heard a funny shuffling noise in the corridor outside. Chloe's face fell. Guiltily she turned to face the door as a girl with shiny long blonde hair hopped into the room. The girl's right foot was in a pink plaster cast and she was walking with the help of crutches. Blossom fled back up to the ceiling.

"Hurry up," said the girl to Chloe. "You're needed onstage."

Blossom was surprised by the girl's unfriendly tone, but she was even more surprised by Chloe's reaction. Chloe's confident manner drained away.

"S-s-s-sorry, Katie," she stuttered. "I was practising my lines."

"Let's hope you get them right," said Katie sweetly. She tapped the floor with her crutch. "You didn't yesterday."

"It was only my second time," Chloe protested.

Katie ignored her.

"I can't believe I broke my ankle,"

she muttered as she left the room. "I was brilliant as Alice. The show's going to be ruined now."

Thinking that Chloe might be about to cry, Blossom fluttered down and landed in the palm of her hand. Chloe brightened and

Blossom was glad she'd acted impulsively. If she'd stopped to think about what she was doing, she'd probably have been too shy to get so close.

"I have to go," Chloe sighed. "It's the dress rehearsal."

Blossom twiddled her wand. This was her chance. She would tell Chloe that she was here to help *her* and sprinkle her with magic good-luck stars. She flew into the air, her wand poised ready to cast her spell, but Chloe was in too much of a hurry to notice. With a quick wave, she rushed from the room.

"Wait!" cried Blossom.

She flew after Chloe but another door opened in the corridor and two children squeezed out of it. They were dressed identically, with massive fake tummies that wobbled when they walked.

"Hi, Chloe," they called as they wobbled towards her.

Blossom followed the trio up one flight of stairs and along another corridor until they were backstage. A large group of children was crowded round a hassled-looking lady clutching a clipboard.

"Alice," she said, ticking her off on a list. "Tweedledum and Tweedledee. Fantastic! Now you're all here we can start. Alice, you're on first."

Someone handed Chloe a book as she nervously went and sat in the middle of the stage. The lady with the clipboard watched from the front. Katie was there, sitting in the second row, her crutches propped up against the seats.

"When you're ready," the lady called.

Blossom flew to the stage and hovered by the curtains. She guessed that the clipboard

lady was the director of the show. Poor
Chloe looked so frightened. Her green eyes
were enormous and when she opened her
mouth to say her first line all that came out
was a croak.

"Come on, Chloe,"
Blossom whispered
encouragingly.

Clearing her throat,
Chloe tried again.

"I'm bored," she sighed,
flicking through the
book. "There aren't any
pictures to look at."

Chloe's acting was
nothing like it had been in her dressing
room. Her body was stiff and her voice
wobbly. Plenty of the cast forgot their lines
and there was lots of giggling as the director
bellowed prompts from the front. But when

Chloe forgot her lines she took it very seriously, blushing furiously, her eyes sliding to Katie who responded with a scowl. Chloe's confidence had ebbed away and the more nervous she became the more lines she got wrong. At the end of the last scene the director sighed heavily as she stood up.

"That was not your best acting," she announced to everyone. "I can only hope that you are saving yourselves for the first performance tomorrow. Chloe, you need to go home and learn your lines."

Tears welled in Chloe's eyes. She hung her head so no one could see her as she rushed back to her dressing room. Blossom raced after her, only just making it into the room before Chloe shut the door.

"I thought you did really well," she said, hovering in front of her.

"Oh! You're still here," said Chloe,

brushing her tears away and managing a small smile. "I was awful. I know my lines off by heart but when I'm onstage I can't remember them. It doesn't matter how hard I practise. I'll never be as good as Katie. She was brilliant. Everyone said so."

"You have to stop comparing yourself to Katie," said Blossom sensibly.

"It's not that easy. Tracy, the lady in charge, is her mum so Katie comes to the theatre every time we rehearse. It's bad enough knowing she's watching without all the mean comments she makes."

"She must be really disappointed to miss out on playing the leading role," said Blossom sympathetically.

"She is," said Chloe, wriggling out of her costume. "But she shouldn't take it out on me!"

Chloe put the dress and apron on to

a coat hanger and hung them in a small wardrobe. Then she slid out of Alice's shoes.

"Where are my trainers? Oh, there they are." Chloe pulled her trainers out from under the wardrobe, jumping back as something rushed past her.

"A mouse!" she squealed.

The mouse ran a full circle round the room before darting back under the wardrobe.

"Wasn't it sweet?" said Chloe, her eyes shining. "Did you see its cute little face? It had the longest whiskers ever. Better not tell Gerry," she quickly added. "He's the caretaker. He keeps this place so clean. He's always sweeping and polishing. He'd have a fit if he knew there was a mouse."

"I wonder why the mouse is living here," said Blossom thoughtfully. There couldn't be much to eat in the theatre if Gerry kept it so clean. She was about to suggest she went and had a chat with the mouse to see if everything was all right when there was a knock on the dressing-room door.

"Chloe, it's Mum. Are you ready, sweetheart? We've got to rush. I said I'd pick Dad up from the station in ten minutes."

Chloe's face fell.

"I don't want to go yet! We've hardly had any time together," she whispered.

Blossom smiled with pleasure. "I don't want you to go either," she said. "But I promise I'll see you again soon."

"Chloe," called Mum. "Please hurry up."

"Coming," Chloe sighed, and grabbed her bag from the floor. "Bye, Blossom. It was brilliant fun meeting you."

Chloe hurried out to
meet her mother. Blossom
hesitated, wanting to check
on the mouse. Suddenly
she remembered she
hadn't sprinkled Chloe
with magic good-luck
stars and tomorrow
was the first day of the
play.

"Honey mites!" exclaimed Blossom,
swishing the air with her wand. How could
she have been so forgetful? She whizzed
along the corridor hoping to catch Chloe
before she left the theatre. But it was too
late. As Blossom flew into the car park
Chloe and her mum were closing their car
doors. Seconds later the engine purred into
life and the car began to move. Dismayed

Blossom watched it go. Now what? She didn't know where the station was or where Chloe lived. If she was braver, she would have chased after the car, but what if she couldn't keep up and got lost? The thought made Blossom's wings tremble.

"I failed!" she groaned.

It was just as Coral had said it would be. Wings drooping with disappointment, Blossom returned to the Crystal Caves.

Chapter Four

In the late afternoon sunshine Firefly
Meadow was a glorious blaze of colour
but even the sight of the sycamore tree, its
outstretched branches welcoming Blossom
home, couldn't lift her spirits. Worse still
Coral was sitting near the squirrel hole in
the shade of a cluster of leaves.

"Well?" she said as Blossom landed. "Did
you pass?"

Sadly Blossom shook her head.

"No, I didn't complete my task."

"Told you so," said Coral, smugly

fluttering her orangey-pink wings. "I don't
know why Miss Alaska gave you that task
when she knew you'd fail."

"What do you mean?" asked Blossom.

Coral narrowed her ice-blue eyes and said spitefully, "Miss Alaska said you wouldn't pass. She didn't think you were brave enough to go through with the task."

"Miss Alaska said that?" exclaimed Blossom.

Coral looked shifty. "Maybe not in those words, but it's what she meant. She said you'd definitely need another day to complete the task. But what if you mess up again? It's the first performance tomorrow. If Chloe doesn't get her good-luck stars, the show will be ruined."

Coral paused to let her words sink in before adding, "I think you should give your task to someone else."

"But that would mean I'd fail," whispered Blossom. "I want to try again."

"Remember the Fairy Bear Promise,"

said Coral sternly. "'I promise to do my best for the *children*', not 'I promise to do my best for myself'."

Blossom twiddled her wand in her paws. Coral was right. Fairy Bears were supposed to put others before themselves. She'd already failed to give Chloe the good luck she needed. What if she didn't succeed a second time? When Blossom looked up, Coral was still staring at her, her blue eyes cold and unfriendly.

Sighing miserably, Blossom headed towards the squirrel hole.

"Where are you going?" called Coral.

Blossom ignored her and flew inside the tree trunk. It was bad enough giving up without sharing the decision with Coral. At first Blossom drifted slowly down the inside of the sycamore tree, delaying the moment when she would have to tell Miss Alaska she couldn't finish her task. But being in the dark was fun, and even though she was feeling sad it made Blossom's fur tingle with pleasure. Her mind drifted to Chloe and suddenly Blossom snapped out of her daydream. There wasn't time to dawdle. School was over for the day. She must catch Miss Alaska before she went home so that she could arrange for another Fairy Bear to take her place. Hoping she wasn't too late, Blossom dived to the bottom of the tree and raced through the Grand Door.

"Please let me get there in time," she muttered, as she flew down the gnarled root staircase and along the Main Tunnel.

The school playground was deserted. Blossom hurried across it and inside the caves. As she neared her class cave, she could hear Miss Alaska talking. Relieved, Blossom slowed, fluttering to the ground.

She leaned against the cave's cool walls
to get her breath back. At last she was
breathing normally but she couldn't stop
her paws and wings from trembling with
nerves. Wondering who Miss Alaska was
talking to, Blossom peeped into the class
cave.

To her surprise Miss Alaska was alone.

"Who's that?" Miss Alaska stopped
talking and stared at the doorway.

"It's me," said Blossom, timidly walking
into the room.

"Come in," said Miss Alaska, clearly
delighted to see her. "I'm rehearsing
a speech to give to the new parents of
the Fairy Bears who will be joining the
school in cub class next term. Would you
mind being my audience? It's all very
well practising on your own but it's quite
another thing speaking in front of others. It

makes me nervous just thinking about it."

"*You* get nervous?" Blossom was astonished.

Miss Alaska laughed. "It's quite natural," she said. "Nerves don't have to stop you from doing the things you want to. They can be very useful. If you're  too confident, then you don't always pay attention to what you're doing and you make mistakes."

Blossom sat on her stone seat to listen to Miss Alaska's talk. When she'd finished, Blossom clapped.

"That was very good," she said bashfully. "You didn't look nervous either."

"Thank you, Blossom," Miss Alaska smiled. "Shall I tell you my secrets for dealing with nerves? First you must remember to take long, slow breaths. When you're nervous, you often take shallow breaths and that makes you feel worse. Breathing deeply is very good for calming the jitters. Next, think to yourself

I *can* do this. If you tell yourself you can do something, then you're more likely to succeed. And, lastly, try to enjoy it. Instead of worrying about what might go wrong, think about what will go right."

"That's a lot to remember," said Blossom.

"It's not really," said Miss Alaska kindly. "Deep breaths, think to yourself I can do this and enjoy. It's simple."

Put like that it did sound simple. Blossom's fur crackled with excitement. Perhaps she would be able to complete her task after all.

"How did you get on today?" asked Miss Alaska.

Blossom hesitated. She'd meant to ask Miss Alaska to give her task to someone else but now she wasn't sure what to do. She knew she should put Chloe before herself but she felt more positive of succeeding with Miss Alaska's helpful tips.

"I found Chloe but I didn't manage to give her the good-luck stars," she said.

Miss Alaska smiled. "Finding Chloe was a good start. Have confidence in yourself, Blossom. I wouldn't have given you this job if I didn't think you were ready for it."

Blossom twisted her wand in her paw. Her stomach was fizzing with anxiety. What should she do? She took a deep breath in and let it slowly out. She took another, and another. After a bit her stomach began to calm down.

I can do this, Blossom thought. I know I can.

And it would be fun. Blossom liked Chloe and wanted to help her.

Smiling up at Miss Alaska she said, "Thanks. I won't let you down. Tomorrow

I'm going to finish my task."

Miss Alaska patted Blossom on the shoulder with the tip of her pink and yellow wing.

"That's the spirit," she said. "Blossom the Brave."

Chapter Five

As she flew home along the cave tunnels, Blossom wondered if she'd made the right decision. But each time she doubted herself she remembered Miss Alaska's delighted face when she'd said she would finish her task. Miss Alaska had great faith in her so she would have faith in herself. Blossom turned off the Main Tunnel and into the one leading to her home cave and was surprised to see Coral. Was she waiting for her? Blossom thought about flying past her but Coral was waving. Reluctantly

Blossom the Brave

Blossom landed beside her.

"Who did Miss Alaska pick to go on the task instead of you?" asked Coral eagerly.

"No one," said Blossom, smiling brightly. "Miss Alaska taught me how to deal with my nerves. I'm carrying on with the task."

Coral folded her wings tightly behind her back and her blue eyes narrowed.

"You," she spluttered. "But . . ."

"I've got to go. It's nearly my tea time," said Blossom, knowing that Coral wasn't happy with her decision. "See you, Coral."

Quickly Blossom stepped round her and flew the short distance home.

That evening Blossom couldn't help worrying about whether she'd made the right decision but she breathed deeply and told herself she had. By bedtime she was exhausted and slept soundly until her alarm clock buzzed her awake early the next morning. There was freshly collected nectar, strawberries and honey biscuits for breakfast. Blossom thought she'd be too anxious to eat but the strawberries were so delicious she managed a whole bowl.

"Good luck," said her mum, hugging

her. "I know you can do this."

Giggling, Blossom wriggled free. It was nice that Miss Alaska and her mum had so much confidence in her. It gave her the courage to prove them right.

The Main Tunnel was very busy. Impatiently Blossom walked behind a large Fairy Bear with enormous red wings. Her stomach was fluttering but she took some deep breaths and felt calmer. Blossom ran her paw along the jewel-studded wall, loving the feel of the magically sparkling gemstones lighting the way. Blossom was nearing the gnarled root staircase when she heard a shout.

"Blossom!"

Turning, she saw Coral a few paces along the Turquoise Tunnel. Blossom waved but Coral seemed upset.

"Please help me," she begged.

Blossom turned into the tunnel.
"What's wrong?"

"I've lost my wand,"
sobbed Coral. "I must
have dropped it
somewhere."

Blossom stared at
Coral in disbelief.

"Why aren't you at
home?" she asked. "It's far too early for
school."

Coral didn't meet Blossom's eye.

"We'd run out of honey for breakfast.
I've just been to the Nectar Cave to get
some."

The Nectar Cave was a swapping
place where the Fairy Bears traded nectar
for honey with the bees. Blossom wasn't
surprised that Coral's family had run out of
honey. Her parents worked long hours for

King Boris and Queen Tania and Coral was often left to fend for herself. Suddenly Blossom felt sorry for her.

"I'll help you look for your wand," she said kindly.

"Thanks, Blossom," said Coral, immediately cheering up. "I think I dropped it on the way to the nectar cave."

Slowly Coral retraced her paw steps. Blossom walked beside her, keeping her eyes on the tunnel floor, looking for the lost wand.

"It's not here," wailed Coral as they arrived at the nectar cave.

"Maybe someone's picked it up," suggested Blossom. "Let's go in and ask."

There was a queue of Fairy Bears inside the cave.

"The bees haven't arrived yet," explained a motherly-looking Fairy Bear with pretty blue wings.

"We're not here for honey," said
Blossom shyly. "My er . . . my friend was
here earlier and now she's lost her wand."

"Has anyone found a wand?" called the
Fairy Bear. "What colour was it, dear?"

"White," said Coral, sniffing. "With a
gold horseshoe set in its star."

The waiting Fairy Bears shook their heads.

"When did you say you lost it?" called the Fairy Bear at the front of the queue. "Only I've been here for ages and I don't remember seeing you."

"It was quite early," mumbled Coral, a pink flush spreading over her white fur. "Thanks anyway."

As she hurried out of the cave, Blossom stared after her. What was going on? Coral had said she'd been to the Nectar Cave to get honey. But how could she when the bees hadn't arrived yet? With a sinking feeling Blossom realized that Coral didn't have any honey with her. Was this a horrible trick to make her late for her task? At once Blossom rushed outside the cave. Coral was already on her way home.

"Wait!" cried Blossom, flying after her.

"What's going on? Have you lost your wand or not?"

Coral's eyes narrowed to mean little slits.

"I just remembered I left my wand at home," she said sweetly. "Silly me!" Thanks for your help, Blossom. I hope I didn't make you too late."

Blossom was so angry! She clenched her paws tightly. The more she thought about Coral's mean trick, the crosser she grew. Blossom took a deep breath. If breathing could help calm nerves, maybe it could help calm her anger too. By her third breath she was beginning to relax. Blossom unclenched her paws.

"Never mind," she said slowly. "Have a good day at *school*. Bye, Coral."

Holding her head high Blossom flew past Coral and made her way as fast as she could to the gnarled root staircase.

Chapter Six

Blossom flew faster than she'd ever flown in her life. She had to get to the theatre in time. There was no way she was failing her task now. She wanted to pass not just for Chloe's sake but to show Coral that her mean behaviour was a waste of time. Blossom flew over the theatre and straight in through the back door. In a funny way Coral had done her a favour. As Blossom sped down the corridor to Chloe's dressing room, she realized that she hadn't had time to feel nervous. Suddenly Blossom heard

footsteps coming down the stairs. She gave
an extra burst of speed, meaning to dive
into Chloe's dressing room before she was
spotted. Then Blossom skidded to a mid-
air halt. The door was closed! She'd come
within a millimetre of crashing into the
green paintwork.

The footsteps were getting closer.
Blossom flew to the bottom of the door
to see if the gap was wide enough for her
to fly underneath but it wasn't. Her heart
began to race. Now what? The safest thing
would be to stay where she was and hope
whoever was coming didn't notice her. Not
many humans looked at
the ground when
they walked.
Blossom watched
the staircase
and soon a foot

appeared in the corridor. It was quickly followed by another and Blossom squeaked in alarm!

Gerry the caretaker was working his way towards her, vigorously polishing the wooden skirting board with a feather duster on a long stick. Blossom was seconds from being swept away. Would Gerry notice her if she made a sudden dash for the ceiling? Then miraculously Chloe's door opened and Chloe, dressed in her blue-and-white Alice costume, stuck her curly head into the corridor.

"Er, hello, Gerry. I was just wondering what that banging sound was."

Chloe quickly shut the door but Blossom was quicker. She whizzed through it and landed on Chloe's dressing table where she collapsed. Her heart was beating furiously and her wings were trembling.

"Blossom!" Chloe sounded delighted to see her. She lowered her voice to a whisper. "Guess what? The mouse we saw yesterday has babies. There's a nest under my wardrobe. I found it this morning when I first came in. The babies must have been hungry. They were squeaking like mad. They can't stay here. Gerry's bound to find them. I was just checking to see if the coast was clear for me to move the nest. There's a park nearby. It's a much better place for a mouse and her family to live."

"Have you got time to do that now?" asked Blossom. The play would be starting soon.

Chloe checked her watch.

"Yes, if I'm quick," she replied.

"I'll help, then," said Blossom decisively. "But let me talk to the mouse first to explain what's happening."

"You can do that?" Chloe was impressed.

Blossom flew under the wardrobe. It was lovely and dark, and as soon as Blossom's eyes had adjusted she spotted the nest. The mouse crouched in front of it, watching Blossom uneasily with twitching whiskers.

Blossom took a deep breath to help with her own shyness.

"Hello," she said.

"Hello," squeaked the mouse in surprise. "How can you talk to me? I thought only adult Fairy Bears could do that."

"Mum and Dad taught me," said Blossom, who loved animals. When she was little she had begged her parents to teach her the magic needed to talk to them. "You're in danger," she continued. "My friend Chloe and I want to help you."

Quickly Blossom explained to the mouse about Gerry the caretaker and Chloe's plan to move her and her family to the park. The mouse was delighted.

"I didn't mean to have my babies here," she explained. "I used to live in a lovely overgrown garden until a family with three cats moved into the house. I was trying to move but got caught in a thunderstorm and came in here to shelter. Then my babies arrived early and I was stuck. They're far too little for me to move them on my own but it's hard living here. It's so clean. There's never enough to eat."

The mouse showed Blossom her three babies. They weren't much larger than Blossom and they all had cute furry faces and long whiskers.

"They're lovely," whispered Blossom.

Proudly the mouse puffed out her chest. "Thank you," she said.

Thoughtfully Blossom made her way back to Chloe. How would they move the nest without damaging it or hurting the babies? The answer came to Blossom in a flash. She flew to Chloe and rested on her hand.

"Can we move the nest in your bag?" she asked.

"Of course," said Chloe. "I'll empty my things out to make more room."

When the bag was empty, Chloe lay on her tummy and stretched her arms under the wardrobe. They were only just

63

long enough to reach the nest. Carefully
she pulled it towards her. The mother ran
alongside squeaking fretfully. Chloe put the
nest in the bottom of her bag then pulled
the side down so the mouse
could climb in beside it.

"Ready?" she said to
Blossom.

Blossom nodded and
flew up to the ceiling
as Chloe opened her
dressing-room door.

The corridor was
empty and Chloe
hurried along it,
holding the bag carefully. As she went
outside, a voice made her jump.

"Where are you going in such a hurry?"

Gerry the caretaker was carefully
cleaning his duster under the outside tap.

"Hello, Gerry," said Chloe, quickly recovering herself. "I need some fresh air. It's so hot in this costume."

"What's the bag for, then?" Gerry asked curiously.

"The bag . . ." Chloe paused and Blossom, hovering a safe distance away, held her breath. How would Chloe explain the bag away?

"The bag is for my play script and a bottle of water," said Chloe. She gave Gerry a conspiratorial grin. "I'm going to the park to practise my lines. It'll be much quieter there. Every time I try to practise here someone disturbs me."

Gerry grinned. "That's a nice idea. Have you got a watch? You won't be late back?"

"And miss my chance to play Alice?" said Chloe. "I promise I won't be late."

With a cheery wave Chloe set out for the park. Blossom flew high in the sky until the caretaker was out of sight then darted back down to Chloe's side.

"You were brilliant," she said admiringly. "You're a born actress."

"Am I?" Chloe was very pleased. "Then why can't I act in front of an audience? I get so nervous that all my lines fly out of my head."

"Nerves can be a good thing," said Blossom, repeating what Miss Alaska had told her the night before. Carefully carrying the mouse and her nest Chloe listened intently to Blossom as she told her Miss Alaska's tips on dealing with nerves.

"So I have to take deep breaths and keep telling myself I *can* play Alice," said Chloe, when Blossom had finished.

"And enjoy it," Blossom added.

A smile spread slowly across Chloe's face. "It sounds quite simple when you put it like that."

Blossom thought about all she'd achieved by taking control of her nerves.

"It is," she said, grinning back.

Chapter Seven

The park was a great place for the mouse to live. As soon as Chloe let her out of the bag she ran around squeaking with delight.

"I'd like to live there," the mouse told Blossom. "Under the bush with the yellow flowers. The prickly leaves will keep my nest safe and in the autumn there'll be juicy berries to eat."

Chloe eased the mouse nest out of her bag. It was very fragile and she didn't want to break it. Blossom fluttered beside her interpreting the mouse's squeaks, telling

Chloe exactly where the mouse wanted her nest. Chloe had to lie on her tummy to push the nest far enough under the bush. At last the nest was safely in position, and the mouse couldn't stop thanking everyone.

"Chloe says you're welcome," said Blossom, this time translating human to mouse. "But we have to go now because she's acting in a show."

"Come and visit me," said the mouse.

"We will," promised Blossom.

Chloe stood up and brushed the dirt from her pinafore.

"I'm filthy," she said, pulling a face.

Blossom the Brave

Chloe was so busy trying to get her apron clean that she forgot to look where she was going. The hem of her dress snagged on a prickly bush and there was loud ripping noise.

"My dress!" she gasped. Her eyes were wide with fright as she took in the torn material. "It's ruined."

Chloe wasn't exaggerating. The white pinafore apron was stained and the blue skirt was ripped. There was no way Chloe could wear it for the performance. Her eyes filled with tears and she sank down on a park bench.

Blossom couldn't bear to see Chloe so unhappy.

"Don't cry," she said, flying down and landing on her hand. "I can fix it."

"How?" Chloe sobbed. "There's not enough time."

"Magic," said Blossom, pointing her wand at Chloe's dress.

"Really?"

Chloe brushed her tears away. "Oh, Blossom, can you do that?" she asked hopefully.

"Yes," said Blossom, trying to sound confident. Mending Chloe's dress would take a lot of skill. Was she able to perform such strong magic? As Blossom pointed her wand at Chloe's dress, her paw was shaking and she had to grip the wand tightly to stop herself from dropping it. Blossom mumbled:

Blossom the Brave

"Wand repair
This horrible tear."

The wand twitched and Blossom gripped it more tightly but only a few small pink stars plopped from its tip. The stars drifted towards Chloe's torn dress but evaporated before they reached it. Blossom gritted her teeth, and repeated:

"Wand repair
This horrible tear."

The wand made a soft hissing sound but this time there weren't any stars. In a panic Blossom waved the wand wildly at Chloe's costume, and chanted:

"Repair, repair, repair,
This horrible, horrible tear."

Nothing! The wand lay lifeless in Blossom's trembling paw. Blossom's tummy was churning so badly it was making her feel sick. Why wasn't her magic working? Then she remembered what Miss Alaska had said yesterday.

"Nerves are awful. They can stop you doing something you want to."

Was that it? Were Blossom's nerves stopping her magic from working? Blossom shook her wings. She took several long deep breaths and felt better. With a slightly trembling paw she pointed her wand at Chloe's dress and said firmly:

"*Wand repair*
This horrible tear."

The wand jerked, its handle grew warm, there was a loud whooshing sound and a fountain of pink stars flowed from its tip and cascaded over Chloe. The blue fabric began to glitter. More stars poured from Blossom's wand until Chloe's dress was crackling with magic.

"Make the apron clean and bright,
From dirty brown to sparkling white,"

Blossom sang confidently.

Gradually the fizzing stopped and the glittering stars faded away. Chloe jumped up and gave a twirl.

"It worked," she gasped. "The magic worked. Blossom, you're brilliant!"

Blossom grinned.

"And you're going to be too," she said. "Come on, Chloe. It's time for you to play Alice."

Back in Chloe's dressing room Blossom

perched on the mirror while Chloe yanked a comb through her hair.

"Shame you couldn't fix this for me," she joked. "It's full of twigs from the bushes in the park."

"Maybe next time," said Blossom, who was quite exhausted from performing such a strong spell.

"Does that mean I get to see you again?" asked Chloe.

"I hope so." Blossom had grown very fond of her new friend. Rallying herself she stood up. There were still two things she had to do. First she had to sprinkle Chloe with good-luck magic, even though Blossom knew she didn't need it any more. Blossom waved her wand, loving the warmth of it glowing in her hand as she chanted her spell.

Fairy Bears

"Good luck to Chloe and everyone.
Make their show lots of fun."

Pink stars fell gently over Chloe, making
her hair and skin sparkle. Chloe put out her
hands to catch them, laughing delightedly
as they fizzled away.

"Thank you, Blossom!" she cried.

"And here's something to remember me
by," said Blossom, concentrating on her
next spell:

"From me to you,
A star that's true."

The wand jerked
as a large pink
star suddenly
burst from its end.
Catching it in both

paws Blossom held out the star to Chloe.

"A friendship star," she said, smiling.

Chloe's green eyes shone with delight.

"It's beautiful," she whispered, carefully putting the star in the pocket of her apron. I'll always remember you, Blossom. And this star will bring me extra luck when I play Alice."

Blossom laughed. "You're going to be fantastic," she said.

Blossom stayed to watch the opening of the play. Chloe was amazing. She didn't seem nervous at all. Blossom could tell she was enjoying herself!

The little Fairy Bear wanted to watch the whole play but she had to get back to school to tell Miss Alaska she'd completed her task. Flying away from the theatre, Blossom was so excited at her own success she turned a series of cartwheels.

"Watch where you're going," cried a butterfly, swerving to avoid a collision.

"Sorry!" said Blossom, quickly righting herself.

She sped home, skimming across Firefly Meadow then soaring up high to reach the squirrel hole hidden in the branches of the sycamore tree. Blossom dived through the hole and floated down the tree's dark insides. She hopped through the Grand Door and jumped down the gnarled root staircase two steps at a time. She arrived back in class panting but happy.

"Blossom's here," called Sparkle excitedly as her friend entered the cave.

Everyone stopped tidying up and stared at Blossom as she made her way to the front of the class. Blossom held her head high, smiling at everyone, even Coral who glared nastily at her as she passed.

Blossom the Brave

"Hello, Blossom," said Miss Alaska. "I can tell from your face that it's good news."

"I completed my task," agreed Blossom proudly.

The class cheered noisily and clapped their wings together. When they'd calmed down, Blossom told everyone about her exciting day. Then Miss Alaska stepped forward.

"Blossom is not only clever and brave,"

she announced. "She is also very modest.
I don't expect many of you knew before
today that she can speak with animals, even
though it's an advanced skill usually learned
in the seniors. I'm very proud of you,
Blossom. Class, let's give Blossom the Fairy
Bear Salute."

Blossom's pale-gold fur turned scarlet
with embarrassment. The Fairy Bear Salute
was only given on very special occasions.

"Deep breath," whispered Miss Alaska,
winking at her.

"And enjoy it," Blossom whispered back.

The little Fairy Bear breathed deeply,
and as the class dipped their wings she *did*
enjoy it!

Blossom

1. Favourite colour – *pink*

2. Favourite gemstone – *pink diamond*

3. Best flower – *pansy*

4. Cutest animal – *mouse*

5. Birthday month – *May*

6. Yummiest food – *honey biscuits*

7. Favourite place – *Diamond Dell*

8. Hobbies – *thinking up stories, talking to animals*

9. Best ever season – *spring*

10. Worst thing – *cruelty to animals*

Blossom's Quiz

I love living in the Crystal Caves, and performing magic is fun! Chose the right word from the list below to answer the Fairy Bear questions.

fly   Promise   honey
tasks   wand   Firefly

1)   The Crystal Caves are hidden underneath a sycamore tree in _ _ _ _ _ _ _ Meadow.

2)   Fairy Bears are about the size of a bumble bee and can _ _ _.

3)   Fairy Bears perform spells by using a magic _ _ _ _.

4)   In the Nectar Cave, we trade nectar for _ _ _ _ _ with the bees.

5)   We chant the Fairy Bear _ _ _ _ _ _ _ every day in school.

6)   Fairy Bears must perform special _ _ _ _ _ so that they can move up to the next class.

A Puzzle for Primrose

Brainy Primrose is stuck! Her task is
to help a sad little dog, but she keeps
seeing Lucy in the magic mirror.
Will she solve the puzzle in time?

Misty Makes Friends

Caring Misty must help Jessica and
her stepsister Becky to become friends.
But first Misty must realize that being
confident isn't easy for everyone . . .

Collect tokens from each Fairy Bears book to WIN!

What prizes can you get?

3 tokens get a Fairy Bears colour poster for your wall!

5 tokens get a sheet of super-cute Fairy Bears stickers!

8 tokens get a set of postcards to send to your friends, plus a certificate signed by the Fairy Bears creator, Julie Sykes!

Send them in as soon as you get them or wait and collect more for a bigger and better prize!

Send in the correct number of tokens, along with your name, address and parent's/guardian's signature (you must get your parent's/guardian's signature to take part in this offer) to: Fairy Bears Collection, Marketing Dept, Macmillan Children's Books, 20 New Wharf Road, London N1 9RR.

Terms and conditions: Open to UK and Eire residents only. Purchase of the Fairy Bears books is necessary. Please ask permission of your parent/guardian to enter this offer. The correct number of tokens must be included for the offer to be redeemed. No group entries allowed. Photocopied tokens will not be accepted. Prizes are distributed on a first come, first served basis, while stocks last. No part of the offer is exchangeable for cash or any other offer. Please allow 28 days for delivery. We will use your data only for the purpose of fulfilling this offer. We will not pass information on to any third parties. All data will be destroyed after the promotion. For full terms and conditions, write to: Fairy Bears Collection, Marketing Dept, Macmillan Children's Books, 20 New Wharf Road, London N1 9RR or visit www.fairybearsworld.com

Fairy Bears Token Offer

1 Token

Prizes available while stocks last. See www.fairybearsworld.com for more details

Fairy Bears Token Offer

1 Token

Prizes available while stocks last. See www.fairybearsworld.com for more details

Fairy Bears

By Julie Sykes

Discover more friendly Fairy Bears!

Dizzy	978-0-330-51201-5	£3.99
Sunny	978-0-330-51202-2	£3.99
Blossom	978-0-330-51203-9	£3.99
Sparkle	978-0-330-51204-6	£3.99
Primrose	978-0-330-51205-3	£3.99
Misty	978-0-330-51206-0	£3.99
Lulu	978-0-330-51207-7	£3.99
Poppy	978-0-330-51208-4	£3.99

The prices shown above are correct at the time of going to press. However, Macmillan Publishers reserves the right to show new retail prices on covers, which may differ from those previously advertised.

All Pan Macmillan titles can be ordered from our website, www.panmacmillan.com, or from your local bookshop and are also available by post from:

Bookpost, PO Box 29, Douglas, Isle of Man IM99 1BQ

Credit cards accepted. For details:
Telephone: 01624 677237
Fax: 01624 670923
Email: bookshop@enterprise.net
www.bookpost.co.uk

Free postage and packing in the United Kingdom